THE CASE OF THE YORKSHIRE TRAIN ROBBERY

The Continuing Chronicles of Sherlock Holmes

C. Thorne

C. Thorne Publishing

ISBN: 9798866640522

Cover and interior page design by: L. Thorne

Library of Congress Control Number: 2018675309
Printed in the United States of America

CONTENTS

INTRODUCTION

Dr. Watson is startled one day by Holmes' news of an audacious train robbery, which occurred overnight on the wind-swept moors of Yorkshire. With haste the pair proceed north only to find the case which lies before them is far stranger than logic or common sense would dictate. Watson wonders aloud why the thieves would have carried out so daring a raid when the jewels aboard the train could have been gotten to in a fart easier manner back in London.

THE CASE OF THE YORKSHIRE TRAIN ROBBERY

I t was a crisp autumn morning some months after my marriage, and my wife was away visiting her cousin in Sussex, who'd given birth to a baby called Albert, after the Prince of Wales, when I received a summons at my home from my dear friend, Sherlock Holmes. I had just settled down to my breakfast with a cup of tea and the morning paper when a note arrived in the hands of a lad of about twelve, its contents enough to rouse me from my comfortable chair and send me hurrying to the hansom cab waiting outside.

The note read:

"Urgent, Watson. Meet me at Baker Street immediately. Bring your service revolver. --- SH"

It was rare for Holmes to resort to such a tone, and as I made my way through the bustling streets of the great metropolis of London, its night fogs still not entirely lifted with the bright sun, I could not help but wonder what had prompted this sudden call to action, though being a former military man, I came ready.

Upon my arrival at my once and future lodgings at 221B Baker Street, I was greeted by Holmes, who was pacing the room with an air of restless energy about him. His piercing eyes darted toward me as I entered, and with a cry of "A-ha!" he handed me a folded newspaper from which a headline blared:

Daring Train Robbery in Wild Dales of Yorkshire

"There you see, Watson, as brazen an example of criminal bravado as exists in the annals of the field! Read on, and see what these 'desperadoes' have achieved."

I knew Holmes did not excite easily and from the tone of his voice and his impatient urging I was primed as I read the article detailing a railroad robbery that had taken place overnight on the London-York express train. A trio of masked men had stormed two cars, first-class and storage, overpowered a pair of armed guards, and made off with a considerable sum of money, valuables....and a cache of priceless jewels en route to the City Museum of York! So skilled and swift were they in their heist that the train never stopped, and most of those aboard beyond the targeted cars knew nothing of what had taken place. The police in rural Yorkshire were caught unprepared, and the passengers had been left in a state of shock.

"It's like the American Wild West come home, Watson!" Holmes cried eagerly.

"Quite the audacious crime," I remarked, finishing the article.

My friend told me: "I have dealt several times, as you know, with thefts which have occurred on trains, the Matter of the Cornish Barrister, as you termed it in your recollection, being a prime example, and always, I might add, I have brought the guilty to justice, but this is new to my experience, a gang being so considerably audacious as to board a moving train and carry out a coordinated heist."

"Yes," I agreed, "the wonder is that no one was left dead, or even seriously injured."

"I sense a matter of some pride in that, Watson, as if the robbers had taken such care to rehearse their larceny that they were determined to achieve their ends without shedding undue blood. It says much about self-perception."

"Well," I said, "that is in their favour, I suppose."

Holmes scoffed, "I give such as these no credit with possessing kindness of heart, Watson, for the have inflicted terror by their deeds, and I can think of several of their victims destined to lose their livelihoods over the matter."

I saw Holmes' eyes take on a faraway cast and he veritably snarled then said, "Enough, Watson. Though the police have not as yet summoned us, I believe they shall, and this case requires our immediate attention. Are you ready this instant to accompany me?"

I said heartily: "Wherever you travel, my friend, I am always ready to trail along!"

Within the space of a quarter-hour we found ourselves in a first-class compartment on the London-York express train, which reminded me of those crimes which had been committed in similar accommodations earlier that night, and as he smoked and considered the facts that were known to him, Sherlock Holmes said to me, "The details of the robbery itself are fascinating, but it is the motive that intrigues me most, Watson."

"Why is that, Holmes?"

"Because it would have been possible to carry out the theft in a much simpler fashion, as the jewels and much else that was ultimately taken were stored the past four days and nights in a warehouse near the Penhallow docks."

"Ah," I agreed, "an easier matter to take the items there than off a train traveling at fifty miles an hour."

"Precisely, Watson."

"And what motivation do you assign that peculiar lack of judgment?"

"I have narrowed it down to a pair of possibilities, Watson. One is simply fame. By that I mean our fellows here, particularly their masked leader, described, incidentally, as 'tall and sturdy and with a hint of the west in his voice,' wished to not merely steal these goods, but to do it in a manner that would give them an incontrovertible claim to legendary status. A blazing American-style robbery committed by boarding a moving train filled with passengers? To travel up and down the cars robbing those they found and making off with the jewels, then exiting while the train remained in motion, and the conductor himself unaware this was even occurring? It is unheard-of!"

"Talk of such an infamous crime would indeed live on for generations," I agreed. "Even the fact such fast horses, actually racehorses stolen from a barn a fortnight ago for the action according to the paper, were needed for the caper shows how much planning and coordination was in place."

"And then the circumstances of the escape, don't forget," Holmes prodded.

"Yes," I said in summation, "the article said this gang carried all this out under so precise a time frame that they were able to exit the train and meet a confederate waiting in a pre-arranged spot, who saw to their escape and disappearance. It is little short of a choreographed miracle, Holmes."

"A masterpiece of cunning and courage, that I will allow, Watson, for though I have no admiration for such flagrant disregard for civilized law, I admit it does impress to think of so much looting coming off without a single apparent mishap."

"You said that was the first possible motive," I reminded him, 'What is the second?"

Holmes paused and a faint flicker of a smile passed for the most fleeting instant across his lips. "Ah, Watson, there I believe I will keep my own confidence for the moment."

Puzzled, I went back to reading my paper.

We rode on in silence for some time after this conversation, but when the train stopped for five minutes in a midlands village called Portonsby, I hopped out to get us each a copy of the morning edition of the local newspaper, and an update of facts revealed more about the purloined gemstones themselves, which I learned were to be displayed for two months at the City Museum of York. In the article was an elaborate history of the gems. The two finest stones, a 30-carat ruby dubbed The Star of Ramapour, and an equally large ruby called The Daughter of the Nile, were worth more in themselves than all else taken.

"Holmes," I pressed my friend, "why did the thieves go to such trouble to rob passengers in first-class, and take other items when these two stones alone could have seen them living in utter luxury til their dying days? What could possibly be more valuable than the gemstones?"

Holmes smiled and nodded, "Ah, after so many years beside me you improve at last in your insightfulness, Watson." "It was the correct question to ask."

"Holmes," I chided, though I was used to him hinting that next to his, my mundane mind was like that of an adolescent.

Then I made a realization. "Somewhere in this is the second possible motive you hinted at, is it not?"

"At present I do not possess enough facts to rule out the more apparent of the motives, straightforward robbery, but, yes, my answer to that, Watson, is that this bold trio may indeed have been after something else on the train, and the theft of the stones, or the robberies of the passengers, or a combination thereof, may have been...." he tossed his hands through the air like an Oriental conjurer, "....smoke and mirrors."

"But what could it have been?"

"That Watson, is the very soul of the mystery. Why indeed, and what indeed? I intend to learn those beguiling answers if it takes all the powers I possess, and all the time remaining to me on this earth. One fact shines a light above all others and cannot be dismissed: the thieves knew exactly what they were after, Watson. They came with *purpose*."

After I considered this second possibility a moment I agreed: "I come to suspect that there is more to this case than meets the eye."

"Ha!" Holmes laughed, pleased. "Watson, there is hope for you yet!"

Our journey through the picturesque countryside was uneventful from that point forward, as I gazed out to see the rolling green pastureland of the midlands gradually transformed into the more rugged northern dales, with their moors and great windy hilltops dotted with hearty breeds of sheep able to weather the temperamental vicissitudes of conditions there, but even as I took in the sights my mind raced back to the unanswered question of motive, which Holmes seemed to think so vital to solving the case. Who were these audacious and skilled robbers, and what had motivated them to target a moving train rather than purloin the precious cargo from a stationary locale? There were, certainly, far easier ways to break the law.

Upon our arrival in Yorkshire just before the hour of noon, Holmes wasted no time in the little village where we found ourselves, roughly twelve miles south of York itself. He hired a swift conveyance to take us out to where the train still sat on the tracks, after finally coming to a stop a mile and a third beyond where the robbers had exited and made off with such expert haste.

We approached the train, which was surrounded by a number of police, both northern constables and what were clearly inspectors brought in from elsewhere, and beyond that there thronged a ring of the curious, and among them all a veritable brigade of newspaper reporters, hungry for this sensational story, which might make their careers.

Holmes pushed past one and all and in the face of an objecting uniformed officer, called out to a familiar figure within the cordon.

"Harvey! My good Inspector Thomas Harvey of York! I have come in anticipation of your summons!"

The inspector, who stood just outside the train, notepad in hand, was a red-haired fellow with side whiskers and thick spectacles. He was less a bulldog in appearance and more the personification of some large, serious feline, perhaps a leopard.

He started upon seeing us and made his way over with a hurried stride, calling, "Holmes, you are both a sight for sore eyes and as ever a shock to my system, as I have only just sent a telegram asking for your aid and did not expect you for hours. I see, however, you have taken the initiative on your own, and for that I heartily thank you! The truth is, in a case like this…well, Mr. Holmes, up here in this lonely spot we need all the help we can get!"

"Thank you, Inspector," said Holmes," for your candor and your welcome. I assure you the sentiment holds meaning, and vow I will do all in my power to bring this matter to conclusion."

I knew my friend often grew annoyed with the disdain he was shown before the public by London police, who were all too eager to receive his assistance in private, but loathe to give him proper credit.

As he walked with us up toward the two train cars where the robbery had been centered, Inspector Harvey blew out his whiskered cheeks and said, "Isn't this a doozy, gentleman? I mean, have you ever seen such a thing? Robbing a moving train so deftly the conductor wasn't even aware and never even slowed down? The whole matter over in minutes and the three perpetrators gone like puffs of smoke into the last hour of night here on the moors!"

With a wave of his gloved hand he indicated the entirety of the wide-open country that surrounded us, making even the bulk of the train feel like a tiny bit of flotsam in a restless ocean.

"That puzzles me," I admitted, taking my opening in the dialog, "unlike in the mountains or forested spots, this country presents few ready-made hiding places. It's very open here for all its sprawling size. Where....did they go?"

The inspector began his reply: "We know they left on horseback, since we've recovered the horses out on the moors, they---"

Holmes interrupted: "They left on a second train."

"What?" Harvey cried. "But there were no other trains running then, Mr. Holmes. I checked that right off."

"No *scheduled* trains, Inspector, but the tracks here, if you observe, are double, north and south, and while I cannot as yet prove this to be our answer, I find it the solution that joins most neatly to the facts. Men on foot could proceed at five miles an hour only, insufficient for escape. Had they continued on the racehorses they acquired to catch the train, that would have given them a speed five times that for a distance of several miles, yet the search of the vicinity of the robbery within ten miles, as I assume has been made, Inspector...?"

"Er, yes," Harvey confirmed, "constables with bloodhounds have sought a distance of ten miles and telegraphs have been sent across the country alerting all to be on watch for these thieves."

"Well there you have it. What then is the answer except a second engine 'borrowed' tonight from a nearby yard, and swiftly returned before it was noticed, waiting in the darkness, stopped and easily unseen by a passing locomotive, a hired accomplice from the railroad itself at the controls, that would convey them at fifty miles an hour and see them far from the scene of the crime before pursuers could begin to draw close. All it took was a little more courage and a jump into the darkness which with practice a man could easily achieve, rolling out of a moving train into the cushioning heather of the moors.

"Something one could do without accruing serious injury," I said, offering my medical opinion. "Bruises at worst."

"You see," Holmes said, "that was their escape, a leap of faith into the darkness, and they were soon gone. A most carefully plotted crime."

"Then now they could be anywhere," Harvey said, dejection in his gruff northern voice. "It may be that by this time they are two hundred miles away."

I pondered what Holmes had told us, and saw the facts fit. The pre-dawn hour, the traumatized state of the passengers leaving them unlikely to see the mask-wearing trio abscond, and the fact the London-York train was moving in the opposite direction would have concealed the presence of a single engine waiting in the night. They would have needed only a few moments at the speed of a train to come to a conveniently arranged point in advance and made their exit there. My friend's genius was a marvelous talent, yet I confess the news made my spirits fall alongside those of the inspector, for how could one hope to apprehend such fellows as these?

Holmes espied our reactions and said, "Be of good cheer, my friends, we have more knowledge than we did even a few moments ago, for now we know *how*, and soon we may know *why*. And now, by your leave, Harvey, I'd like to visit the interior, were the gems were stored and the crimes carried out."

Harvey admitted us up into the car for first-class, which Holmes paced through only once, then proceeded into the storage car where the jewels had been placed in a locked compartment which anyone could clearly see had been busted open by tools wielded in an expert hand. Though Holmes spent several minutes examining the lock under a lens, peering intensely at it, in fact, when he moved on it seemed to me his interest here on the train had been sated.

"Nothing to be found here," he said, confirming my suspicions. Then he asked: "All the passengers are available for interview, should I require them, Inspector?"

"Yes," said Harvey, "though a few, two older ladies and a gentleman who claims he has a heart condition, have been taken into town to be seen by a doctor there. But even those are not going anywhere yet. My men have been conducting interviews and taking statements all morning and have nearly finished with all of them…the whole complaining lot."

"They will have little to add," Holmes predicted. "I think you will find they are one and all genuine victims in this affair. Furthermore, I foretell they shall very soon be reunited with the lost goods which were cruelly stolen away from them."

"You are so confident of success? Harvey asked, clearly impressed.

"There is an odd development ahead," Holmes predicted, sounding proud and earnest. "Have your men search continue to search on the open ground beginning several miles down from the tracks. Look for gunnysacks, and in them I believe will be all that was purloined from first-class. The pocket watches, the ladies' necklaces and rings, even the money. As for the gems," he shrugged. "Those are another story."

"Yes, I understand, the gemstones were the real object," said Harvey.

"Of that I am not sure," said Holmes. "Though as I am working from the assumption that our mastermind used them as payment for his confederates in the crime, and I suspect they shall prove harder to recover, though if you find the two henchmen, you may find each of them with a rare and precious stone in his keeping as recompense for his participation in this singular affair."

"Not with the mastermind…?" Harvey asked. "So the leader of the gang…?"

"Had his own singular agenda and certainly parted almost at once from his fellows, possibly even leaping once again into the night from the second train, even as his hirees would have been celebrating with relief their great criminal triumph."

"Hirees?" quizzed Harvey. "So they were not a gang with a one-for-all mentality?"

"I think," said Holmes, "you will find the two henchmen were selected for certain skills they brought to the table, men of professionalism who drilled with the leader for days, weeks, until they could do as their temporary employer asked of them, moving onto and through a train with all the precision of stage actors undertaking roles. And for their parts they were handsomely paid."

"In jewels," I summed up, grasping the matter as laid out by Holmes.

"But as for the objective of our mastermind, the man who plotted this matter, who hired his confederates, who proceeded with such courage and utter confidence...there I cannot yet say what motivated him, though there was something on this train, Inspector Harvey, Watson, which our leader wanted with a mad passion, something he valued even above gemstones, and certainly above the pocket money stolen from the passengers."

"And why then did this fellow rob the passengers at all? He had the jewels by then."

"Elementary, Inspector...one of the passengers had something he wanted very dearly. Something with a price literally beyond rubies."

"But what?" Harvey asked, dazzled, as was I, by this new wrinkle to what had originally seemed such a straightforward, albeit audacious, crime.

"That we may soon know," said Holmes. "In fact…" his eyes took on a hawkish glint, "I think a new development catches my notice, and I identify an inside man who of necessity aided our bold criminals."

"What?" Harvey cried, gazing about, excitement on his face. "Where?"

Holmes said, "Careful now. You see the employee of the train company who stands off by himself near the engine?"

My eyes moved with the inspector's in the direction toward which Holmes nodded, closer to the fore of the train.

Holmes clarified: "The fellow wearing gray overalls under his coat, with his restless hands in his pockets. I have had my eye on him for the last several minutes, as he stood out in my sight as one acting in ways he should not were he upset by the events of the night. Look around, where others wait breathlessly, feeling lucky to be alive, he…well it is as you see. He is eager. As for whom our mystery figure is, I perceive from a distance that he is a Yorkshire man, that he has no wife at present, and that he conceals some great anticipation which he holds to be to his benefit. He reminds me, Watson, Harvey, of a boy on the eve of Christmas!"

"Like getting a payoff for some role in last night?" Harvey asked.

"Indeed. Mark his reaction, gentlemen, it is less that of a disturbed man than that of an impatient one. He would much sooner be on his way but is prevented by the police ordering everyone to stay here. Yet notice how he remains so close to hand where the police are, listening and observing?"

"Let us go and have a little word with him," Harvey said with a happy growl.

This is exactly what next occurred, and while at first the railroad man, Bill Barker by name, denied any involvement in the affair of the robbery, under the dogged questioning of Inspector Harvey and the occasional revelation of insight from Holmes himself, the fellow broke, and while he pleaded that he did not know there was to be a robbery, he admitted that some weeks previous he had been approached in a dark, crowded pub in York by a man clearly in disguise, who promised he'd be sent twenty pounds for his cooperation in a matter at some future date.

"All I had to do and all I did do, I vow," said Barker, "was wait for a letter which would contain a phrase 'a king shall be born' and it would tell me of this mysterious task I had to do. And it did happen, the promised letter arrived, and so I knew this journey was the one appointed for my mysterious task, which was so simple a thing I almost laughed to see it asked of me."

"Which was?" demanded Holmes.

Barker said, "I had to look out for one man in particular and mark which car in first-class he entered, and unlock the door to that car at a point stated in the letter."

"And which point was that?" Holmes asked him.

"Two miles after we passed the town of Durnby, which we did a few miles back."

"Ah," said Holmes, nodding, "Durnby! That narrows it down a bit. A very good stretch of land for lying in ambush follows Durnby. And what of the passenger whose arrival you marked before unlocking the door? Tell me of him."

Barker described an ordinary chap who could have been any number of men, but Holmes listened attentively and smiled. "Inspector, Watson, this man has just told us a clue of infinite value."

Seizing on the hope in Holmes's words, the inside accomplice, Barker, told him heatedly, "And that is all I did do. I played no role in the robbery, nor, I vow, did I know there'd even *be* a robbery, and was as startled by it as anyone else aboard when it took place!"

"Oh, no," Harvey said sarcastically, "you thought being offered so large a sum of money to unlock the door on a moving train would have no connection to anything which might occur thereafter, did you? Why it was as innocent an undertaking as could be."

Barker's previous look of hopefulness evaporated now that he had been exposed by the great consulting detective as an accomplice in so massive a crime.

Holmes gazed at Barker and told Inspector Harvey, "Yes, he attempts to downplay his own participation when surely he was aware some action would follow his misdeed, but I think this scoundrel knows nothing more of use to us. His knowledge is spent, and I am done with him."

Harvey turned to a bald-headed rural constable who had stood beside him listening, and said, "Charge him in the name of the Queen with being an accomplice in this crime and take him away."

Holmes was already striding off toward the first-class car where most of the victims of the robbery were seated, waiting for police investigating the crime to send them away. He gazed among them for a few instants and then zeroed in on a man matching Barker's description, whom he approached and to whom he politely introduced himself.

"And I am Mr. Charles Welles," the man said back to him, his voice squeaky with so much nervous exertion.

Holmes asked if Welles would mind stepping outside with him for a moment to assist him in his inquiries, and when this was done he asked him, "You are, I believe, employed in some capacity at the City Museum of York?"

"Indeed, yes, sir," Welles replied eagerly and with no small hint of pride, "it is my greatest joy to be a sub-assistant curator of ancient domestic artifacts, and sub-rare domestic acquisitions."

"And for how long have you held this position, Mr. Welles?" Holmes asked.

"Four years now, since I was promoted up from volunteer cataloger. Oh, sir, my mother was so proud of me for moving up like that!"

There was, I found, something in the man's simple earnestness which I liked, and Holmes too seemed disposed to treat him with courtesy.

"I know last night's events were of an upsetting nature to you and to all who fell victim to them," Holmes said, "yet I must ask you to please disclose to me the contents of the museum's case you carried with you, and which sat on the seat beside you before it was purloined in the robbery."

Here Welles hesitated and his eyes moved among us before he sighed and seemed to make an internal decision. "I am reticent to speak of museum matters with outsiders....but I suppose since there was nothing of value entrusted to me, I can answer."

"We do thank you," said Holmes with grave and patient courtesy.

"Foremost in the case were papers relating to instructions about the set-up of displays when we arrived back in York. There were also some small flint arrowheads of the sort so common in man's primitive past, a copper arm spool from a collection acquired on this trip, a paper describing the process of the preparation of dyes in the Bronze Age, and a small round of sandstone of no particular worth about the size of a man's palm, containing a hole through the center, the thing known as the 'Somerset Stone,' found there in that county in a dig during the summer a year ago."

I saw some great change take part in Holmes. "The Somerset Stone!" he repeated. "I thank you, indeed, Mr. Welles."

He walked quickly away, leaving it for a puzzled Harvey to thank Welles and instruct him to return to his seat, and for he and I to trail after Holmes, who moved toward the field in a mode of concentration and satisfaction.

"Gentlemen!' he cried when we caught up to him. "It is clear to me now. The Somerset Seer's Stone! Have you heard of it? No? That simple sandstone disk, *that*, my friends, that was what this entire affair was about!"

"Not the rubies, not the cash taken from the passengers, but a piece of common sandstone?" Harvey challenged, almost sounding as if he doubted what my friend was saying.

"Common? No, Inspector, uncommon indeed, and I think our Mr. Welles, however dedicated to his work he may be, had no idea what item he beheld. I have referred you often, Watson, to myths and legends and their importance as vehicles of truth, and have urged you to make a useful study of them. This is a case where a legend can tell us a good deal. It is what I suspected all along, that our mastermind cared nothing for wealth, he was after something of personal meaning. And now we know it was the stone!"

He seemed to re-gather himself and said, "I see the name means nothing to either of you, but gentlemen, speed is of the essence if we are to apprehend our man, for I know where he is headed, and what he seeks to do. I believe the train company has placed at our disposal anything which might aid our investigation, yes? Then Inspector Harvey, be good enough to request they send us their fastest available engine *at once*. We have a journey ahead of us, and with haste we might yet make up for lost time, and soon be in the footsteps of our prey. The quarry is flushed from the underbrush at last..."

The next hour was a blur of preparation and impatient waiting, in which time a constable informed Inspector Harvey that as Holmes had predicted, a search of the moors some several miles distant had turned up the sacks containing the possessions stolen from the first class passengers.

"Then all went exactly as I deduced," said Holmes, satisfied.

The requested fast train was brought to us, and Holmes bade its crew to travel with all speed, something they were glad to do, reaching seventy miles an hour for much of our journey southwestward, toward, as Holmes informed us, the hill of Glastonbury, for on our way Holmes had told Inspector Harvey and myself everything, and it made for a shocking and singular tale.

"The Somerset Stone," he began, "as it was unimaginatively dubbed by the archaeologists who uncovered it last year, is a wondrous find, indeed, though misidentified, I'm afraid. It is in truth an unparalleled example of an ancient seer's stone, a device of vast importance in the ritual life of Celtic times."

"I am not an academic sort, so I know nothing of these objects, Harvey said, apologetically, frowning.

Holmes told him, "Nor any reason you should, Inspector! In that legendary age, when a great hero was, through his bravery in undertaking some mighty feat of strength or skill or sheer audacity, deemed worthy of reward for his courage, a wizened druid would take him to any of a number of sacred places, like Stonehenge, or Avebury, or the Tor of Glastonbury, and place a ritual seer stone, marked with runish symbols believed imbued with magic, upon his forehead, awakening the third eye and allowing him to see into the otherwise invisible realm of the fey, said to lie beyond mortal senses. The myths say such a hero would then be called by the queen of *Tír na nÓg*, and offered a chance to travel there each night in his waking dreams, and reign beside her for the duration of his lifetime, enjoying adventures and delights the which this earth could not offer."

"Why, that's but a legend," I said.

"A legend it seems our mastermind believes, Watson, as countless thousands have felt reason to believe long before him. Since the stone was found in Somerset County, it was a simple matter to deduce it was linked to the great holy site there, Glastonbury Tor, a place of power and ceremony across perhaps a hundred generations, atop which ceremonies to reward a great hero took place in olden times."

"Good Heavens," breathed Harvey. "So he's a mad man."

"Who's to say?" quizzed Holmes. "But, gentlemen, if we are swift and if we are lucky, we might yet be present when our fellow undertakes his a ritual there in Glastonbury, for he intends to meet his fairy queen."

"The mode of robbing a moving train, like a bandit in the American west," I said, "rather than a more conventional robbery, it was this man's way of proving himself a bold hero! It was the missing fact you puzzled over earlier, Holmes!"

"Precisely, Watson, it all comes clear. This man needed accomplices, and found them. He audaciously stole racehorses needed to catch up with the train, arranged for a locomotive to be taken for a few hours for his retreat after the crime, yet he gave away the rubies as payment to his hired accomplices, discarded goods stolen from the passengers doubtless amounting to some scores of pounds, but which was only a pretext for rifling through the car to find the briefcase held by our Mr. Welles. When the job was done he abandoned his accomplices to their own fates and made off for the southwest here, where he hopes to undertake this ritual, and spend his dream time in the court of a fairy queen!"

"A very odd case," Harvey scoffed, "but I'll grant you a remarkable one at that. I never would have seen it leading here."

Before sunset we arrived in Somerset at the bucolic town of Glastonbury, and with haste Inspector Harvey thunderously ordered a half-snoozing cabbie to put it to the horses and get us out to the tor with all haste.

"If you do there's an extra ten shillings in it for you," promised Holmes in a more soothing tone than the overeager Harvey had employed.

The man complied, whipping his poor horses the whole distance out from town and through the venerable countryside, so steeped in Celtic legend, the tor looming before us, visible for miles in any direction, a conical hill perfect in its formation, its connection to the ritual life of ancient times quite fascinating to ponder.

"I see him!" Harvey shouted. "I see our man!"

As did Holmes and I. The master of the train robbery was kneeling atop the tor, shirtless and barefoot, while an old man with a long unkempt beard, clad in a gray robe of coarse woven wool stood over him with---I espied---the seer's stone pressed to his own heart. As we leaped from the coach and ran on foot up the hill, the old man passed the stone to a young man, no older than twenty-five, I thought, who rose with it in his hand and held it to his forehead. Instantly his face changed, becoming brighter, as if in awe. Midway up the tor and charging, my breath ragged, I heard the man say:

"Yes, Queen Maeve, yes, I behold you and your court! Yes, Queen Maeve, beloved of my soul, I accept! I accept! I am your consort and your champion til the end of my days!"

The man laughed long and hard with sheer delight so animalistic and lost unto itself that I felt a chill to hear it.

The man lowered the stone and as the old fellow in druidic garb stepped away from our approach, he stayed rooted to the spot on top of the great hill, his face the very image of ecstasy.

"You've come too late," the train robber finally said, smiling at us, "and what you do to me now doesn't matter. She's accepted me, you see. Her hero. I'll visit each night in my dreams, and I'll dine at her table, and I'll lie in her arms. I'll live my sleeping nights til the end of my days in a place none of you can begin to imagine."

"Then you'll do it from a gaol cell!" Harvey growled. He slapped handcuffs on the man, and the seer stone, a simple thing to look at, truthfully, fell to the sacred ground. "I arrest you in the name of the Queen, and do charge you with train robbery and a half-dozen other offenses of theft and... Bah! Much else we'll sort out in time."

A few minutes later constables from town, whom Harvey had summoned to meet us, arrived, and the old man, the "druid" (he certainly looked the part, I admitted), was taken into custody as well. There was, I noted, a dignity in the old man's silence that struck me as somehow removed from his circumstances altogether. He too was a believer in other realms, I intuited, and seemed in awe of what he and the "hero" had done that day.

A half hour later found us at a small brick stationhouse, where our fellow and the old druid sat shackled at a table, the latter now looking quite tired after so much nervous energy, but our jaunty train robber giving every appearance of radiant joy, not caring in the slightest that he was in police custody with a long prison sentence looming ahead of him.

Seeking a few final clarifications, Holmes spoke to him, asking about what he had done.

"I could have taken the stone from the London museum at any hour," the young man who identified himself as Harold Dowd, told us, "but that was not the act of the great hero I had of necessity to become if I wished to gain Queen Maeve's attention."

"You who grew up in these parts, the great west-country of our nation," Holmes said, "were raised, I conjecture, hearing tales of the fey lands of ancient times, of the Celts and their era, told you by your mother, who came from an old family?"

"Oh, yes," the man, Harold Dowd admitted. "I loved my mother dearly, and lost her at a young age, but her stories lived on in me, and I never doubted them. They sustained her all her life, passed on to her through her family with its roots so deep in these hills, and they sustained me as well. I thought of the tales night and day, the stories of the great Celtic heroes, and of the magic realms that lay underfoot and in the air itself, unseen. How I desired with all my soul to go to them…"

"It was your mania," I said, in my opinion as a medical man.

"A mania, Doctor?" Dowd scoffed. "No, a religion venerable when the world was new, and this old man, this druid, was my high priest."

"A con man more like it," Inspector Harvey scoffed.

Harold Dowd paid him no mind but seemed driven to explain himself to Holmes. He said:

"I knew one day I must become a hero fulfilling a quest to earn my way into that other realm, yet what that quest would be I was never sure, though I sought one so I might become the consort of a fairy queen. When I heard the stone had been found last year, oh, I desired it, for I knew what it was better than those fool archaeologists, unbelievers and unlearned men, and I knew what it could do for me. So I came up with my idea, using the inheritance I received from my father, a brewery baron here in the west country, to make it all happen. I knew the task called for bravery, but I never shirked my part. I'd rob a train in the American fashion, and seize what I desired. I ask you, Mr. Holmes, have you ever heard of a braver undertaking?"

"Perhaps not," Holmes admitted. "Or a more tragic one. You'll spend the remainder of your days in prison, I wager you."

"You think I care about that?" Harold Dowd laughed a genuine and untroubled laugh. "It doesn't matter where my body goes through its days, in a palace or in a dungeon, not when my nights, I assure you, will be spent in a reverie beyond your wildest imaginations. And in that other realm, sir, those single nights might last *centuries....*"

Harvey thanked my friend for his assistance in bringing to a conclusion one of the most brazen and ultimately odd crimes in a generation, and the train company conveyed us back to London in it most illustrious railroad coach, one reserved in normal times for the use of Dukes and great heads of industry.

As we traveled, tired now after so long a day, we spoke of the events and of the motivation that compelled Harold Dowd to do as he did.

"Belief, Watson," Holmes said, "is indeed the most powerful force in human life. Belief will compel a man to go to the pyre a martyr, or convince him to make a barefoot pilgrimage halfway across the world. And it will convince a man to rob a train and send himself to a prison cell in exchange for a greater reward he believes due to him."

"He..." I paused almost hesitant to add what I wished to note. "He seemed very certain, didn't he?"

"He believed that through the hole in the stone he saw the thing he wished to see," Holmes agreed. "At least for the moment it made him drunken with joy, so intoxicated that even Her Majesty's prisons held no dread for him."

"The mind can delude most powerfully," I said, thinking of numerous medical cases.

Holmes fell silent a moment and I knew his thoughts mirrored my own. What if there was more to greater reality than science or logic could ever prove. *What if?*

In the days ahead, while whoever had driven the getaway train remained unidentified, the two accomplices to the robbery were apprehended, one when he attempted to sell his ruby to a merchant in Bristol who worked as a police informer, and a second when he killed a man in a knife brawl, when the other man tried to take his ruby from him, perilously entranced by its beauty and value. *It glows so brightly,* had been his final words.

"It is," Holmes said, "the destructive nature of unearned wealth, and the metaphorical curse that lies within any great stone. Track their histories and you find a trail of tragedy, sparing neither queen nor commoner. Such jewels, Watson, bring nothing good to any lives they touch, for there is inside grand gemstones the fatal allure of a hooded cobra."

With that, he took down his Stradivarius and noted, "I think a little Brahms would prove soothing tonight?"

Then, with great expertise, my friend began to play.

ABOUT THE AUTHOR

C. Thorne

C. Thorne is an writer who lives in the United States. He is multi-authored and published, having even more tomes beneath his belt through the years as ghostwriter for professors and doctoral students alike. These are his most recent volumes in a series of Sherlock Holmes books.

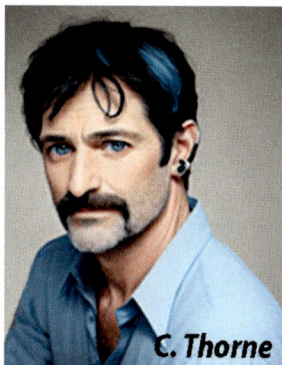

C. Thorne

In addition to his extensive schooling, C. Thorne is a "Road" Scholar, having learned much from life. He hopes you buy and enjoy these and all the books written by C. Thorne and illustrated by L. Thorne, as much as they have enjoyed producing them.

BOOKS IN THE SERIES

In "The Continuing Chronicles of Sherlock Holmes," previously unknown cases from the great consulting detective's career are rediscovered, each faithfully recorded and narrated by Holmes' friend and colleague, Dr. John H. Watson. We hope you'll come along on these newly released accounts detailing adventures amid amazing, ever-remarkable, and occasionally sordid mysteries that arise on the cobbled streets of London, the deceptively placid English countryside, and in genteel estates behind whose imposing facades dark secrets sometimes lie. Striving for an authentically classic tone to these stories, lifelong Holmes fan C. Thorne is proud to present these cases Watson set to pen, but for some reason never released in his lifetime. And now you can be among the first to read them all. Dive deep into another age, another world, another adventure from the life of the greatest detective ever to peer through a magnifying glass, as we give you "The Continuing Chronicles of Sherlock Holmes"!

Sherlock Holmes And The Case Of The Yorkshire Train Robbery

Dr. Watson is startled one day by Holmes' news of an audacious train robbery, which occurred overnight on the wind-swept moors of Yorkshire. With haste the pair proceed north only to find the case which lies before them is far stranger than logic or common sense would dictate. Watson wonders aloud why the thieves would have carried out so daring a raid when the jewels aboard the train could have been gotten to in a far easier manner back in London.

Sherlock Holmes And The Case Of The Slain Newsman

While working in his Harley Street medical office, Watson is stunned to receive word that a promising young crime reporter, with whom Sherlock Holmes had successfully collaborated on some of his recent cases, was found brutally murdered in an alley in the Limehouse District of London's East End, plunging Holmes into ruthless pursuit of his killer.

What exactly had the newsman uncovered in his latest investigation that would motivate person or persons unknown to so viciously take his life in order to cover up dark secrets?

Come along with Holmes and Watson as they find themselves on the trail not only of one man's murderer, but something larger and darker than either had theretofore begun to suspect...

Sherlock Holmes And The Case Of The Condemned Man

Dr. Watson would call it Sherlock Holmes' darkest and most haunting case...the evening Baker Street was visited by a young woman who came alone, pleading for aid in saving her father, an innocent man, she claims, from the gallows in a mere seven days, and in so doing, taking the great detective and his faithful chronicler down a twisted pathway to truth.

From a gloom-filled murder scene in the heart of the city, to the dismal corridors of Reading Gaol, and into the complex and often-cold mind of Sherlock Holmes himself, here tragedy and hope collide in the swirling London fog of long ago.

Sherlock Holmes And The Case Of The Condemned Man

Dr. Watson would call it Sherlock Holmes' darkest and most haunting case...the evening Baker Street was visited by a young woman who came alone, pleading for aid in saving her father, an innocent man, she claims, from the gallows in a mere seven days, and in so doing, taking the great detective and his faithful chronicler down a twisted pathway to truth.

From a gloom-filled murder scene in the heart of the city, to the dismal corridors of Reading Gaol, and into the complex and often-cold mind of Sherlock Holmes himself, here tragedy and hope collide in the swirling London fog of long ago.

Sherlock Holmes And The Case Of Cromwell's Cranium

In this fourth volume of The Continuing Chronicles of Sherlock Holmes, Holmes and Watson are visited at Baker Street by an academic who claims his school's most treasured secret possession, no less than the mummified head of the Lord Protector of England, Oliver Cromwell, has been stolen from his office. As Holmes' investigation takes him from the streets of London, to the rolling downs of Suffolk, to the thriving holiday town of Brighton read along as the world's greatest consulting detective attempts to pierce the mystery of how, when, and by whom England's most long-sought human artifact was taken.

Sherlock Holmes And The Case Of Oscar Wilde's Manuscript

Leave behind the hectic pressures of the present-day and return for a little while to the era of Queen Victoria's storied reign, as on Boxing Day 1894, one of the most celebrated men in all London, the famed writer Oscar Wilde, pays a call at 221B Baker Street, bringing distressing news of a theft which stands to see the manuscript for a novel he dubs nothing less than his magum opus, released before the world under the name of a dastardly plagiarist. Wilde's plea for aid soon has Sherlock Holmes on the trail of this missing treasure of high literary art, setting himself up against a mystery which takes him into the presence of one whose cold-hearted nature threatens to destroy everything it touches.

Sherlock Holmes And The Case Of Revenge At A Wedding

"It is the mystery not the object," Holmes explains to Watson on the morning he is summoned to find the whereabouts of a missing wedding cake to be served at the reception of one of the most celebrated society events of the season. Heading out at once through the Surrey countryside to the estate of a nearly extinct noble family, Holmes soon finds that sinister undercurrents belie the idyllic setting of what the bride's mother, the dowager Lady Prudence describes as the happiest day of her daughter's life.

Sherlock Holmes And The Case Of The Faceless Dutchman

One year after the puzzling case that would go on to be known as The Hound of the Baskervilles, Sherlock Holmes of Baker Street again finds himself confronted by a mystery surrounded by claims of preternatural events, when a young lady becomes caught in a living nightmare which began after her visit to a museum exposed her to the presence of a black marble sculpture of a Renaissance angel, tainted by a long and sinister history. Will this episode of unnatural torment in the heart of London prove the one instance out of an entire career in which cold logic may not triumph, and the diabolical defy the powers of even the world's greatest consulting detective? Find out in The Case of the Faceless Dutchman!

Sherlock Holmes And The Case Of The Intuitive Irregular

On a quiet morning in 1882, early on in Sherlock Holmes' and Dr. John Watson's long and eventful friendship, what began as an ordinary day in the thriving heart of London is changed by the arrival of one of Holmes' legion of street urchins, young Charlie Toppet, among the most colourful of the "Baker Street Irregulars," who act as the great detective's eyes and ears on the streets of the city. Soon caught up in the boy's account of a mysterious figure living alone in a shunned house near the river, a wary and isolated stranger who with an almost ritualistic dedication throws a sack filled with unknown contents into the Thames each day at precisely the same time, out of curiosity Holmes investigates, only to be caught up in what transforms into a matter of personal honour for the world's great detective, still several years removed from his well-deserved fame…. "The Case of the Intuitive Irregular" is the eighth installment in C. Thorne's The Continuing Chronicles of Sherlock Holmes.

Sherlock Holmes And The Case Of The Jousting Yard Ransom

What begins with a pleasant Saturday evening gathering at the home of Dr. and Mrs. Watson, where Sherlock Holmes relates a solo case undertaken in a graveyard in the English Midlands, gives way on Monday to an ardent plea for Holmes' help in returning a young kidnapping victim to her terrified parents. The only clue at the investigation's start is a harsh ransom note in which the brutal abductors vow to send back one of the girl's fingers should outsiders be brought into the case. Making haste to the home of a learned astronomer and his wife in a rural village east of London, Holmes and Watson plunge into "The Case of the Jousting Yard Ransom," the puzzling ninth tale in The Continuing Chronicles of Sherlock Holmes....

Sherlock Holmes And The Case Of The Shadow Of Whitehall

What promises to be a tranquil evening in the early years of Holmes and Watson's time at Baker Street is interrupted via a letter sent by a curator at the British Museum, who rather imperiously demands Holmes appear before him that night in the museum's archives, and lend aid to what he describes as a threat to his honour, and perhaps his very life. Plunging out into the intemperate night, Watson joins Holmes as he enters into the vast after-hours reaches of the world's largest museum, and there, in the darkness, meets a man whose secret past stands in contrast to the circumstances of his present occupation as curator of the institution's Wellington Collection. Soon Holmes is to hear of the malfeasance of a seemingly omniscient blackmailer, a nameless individual whose demands strike at random moments, and whose intention seems to be no less than the ruination of a client whom Holmes realizes is himself not who or what he appears to be.... It's all within The Case of the Shadow of Whitehall, tenth volume in The Continuing Chronicles of Sherlock Holmes.

Sherlock Holmes And The Case Of The Divine Miss Sarah

Who can resist the appeal of a beautiful woman pleading for assistance after an object she held as among her most precious possessions is mysteriously stolen? And what if that woman happens to be the most celebrated actress in Victorian London? Still recovering from a heartbreaking loss that nearly destroyed him, Dr. Watson is called to return to Baker Street as he ventures beside Holmes into a vast West End theater filled with odd characters and strange clues, all in pursuit of a truth that might be less welcomed by the esteemed client than she may care to face. Looming over all are hints of a previous investigation in which the lady played a role, and which clearly left Holmes with a less than approving opinion of some matters from her chequered past. It's all in The Case of the Divine Miss Sarah, the eleventh volume in The Continuing Chronicles of Sherlock Holmes....

Sherlock Holmes And The Case Of Moriarty's Betrayer

Confronted with a development he'd long dreamt of, a weak link in the iron-hard chain of Professor Moriarty's criminal empire, Sherlock Holmes undertakes a series of quests which arise from clues left in a number of locations around London, each message leading onto the next, and in order to keep a prearranged meeting with the mysterious informant who has sent the challenge, the great detective must unravel a complex series of psychological puzzles before he can keep his rendezvous with the unnamed defector. It's all in The Case of Moriarty's Betrayer, the twelfth volume in The Continuing Chronicles of Sherlock Holmes

Omnibus One : The Continuing Chronicles Of Sherlock Holmes

Don your deerstalker cap and escape back to a late-Victorian yesteryear amid the melodious notes of a well-tuned Stradivarius, with The Continuing Chronicles of Sherlock Holmes: Omnibus One, whichbrings together the first eight stories in the ongoing accounts of a number of Holmes' adventures that were until recently lost to time, only to be rediscovered in our own age. Travel along from the dark heart of Whitechapel, and to the wide-open moors of Yorkshire.... Read of an allegedly cursed statue inside a Neo-Gothic museum.... Enter a decaying house beside the

Thames whose walls are covered with strange runic symbols.... Make your way to a tragedy-marked wedding outside a decrepit manor in the rolling hills of Surrey.... And stand atop an ancient Celtic holy site, as these and other stories take readers away in time to the swirling fog of cobbled London streets, as Holmes pursues murderers and thieves, rights the wrongs he finds around him, and peers into the secret hearts of his fellow man, always with the faithful Dr. John H. Watson at his side. This omnibus includes the stories: The Case of the Yorkshire Train Robbery; The Case of the Slain Newsman; The Case of the Condemned Man; The Case of Cromwell's Cranium; The Case of Oscar Wilde's Manuscript; The Case of Revenge at a Wedding; The Case of the Faceless Dutchman; and The Case of the Intuitive Irregular in their entirety, assembled together for the first time ever. We hope you'll journey along, for between these covers, the game is always afoot....

Omnibus One: The Continuing Chronicles Of Sherlock Holmes The Paperback

Don your deerstalker cap and escape back to a late-Victorian yesteryear amid the melodious notes of a well-tuned Stradivarius, with The Continuing Chronicles of Sherlock Holmes: Omnibus One, whichbrings together the first eight stories in the ongoing accounts of a number of Holmes' adventures that were until recently lost to time, only to be rediscovered in our own age. Travel along from the dark heart of Whitechapel, and to the wide-open moors of Yorkshire.... Read of an allegedly cursed statue inside a Neo-Gothic museum.... Enter a decaying house beside the Thames whose walls are covered with strange runic symbols.... Make your way to a tragedy-marked wedding outside a decrepit manor in the rolling hills of Surrey.... And stand atop an ancient Celtic holy site, as these and other stories take readers away in time to the swirling fog of cobbled London streets, as Holmes pursues murderers and thieves, rights the wrongs he finds around him, and peers into the secret hearts of his fellow man, always with the faithful Dr. John H. Watson at his side. This omnibus includes the stories: The Case of the Yorkshire Train Robbery; The Case of the Slain Newsman; The Case of the Condemned Man; The Case of Cromwell's Cranium; The Case of Oscar Wilde's Manuscript; The Case of Revenge at a Wedding; The Case of the Faceless Dutchman; and The Case of the Intuitive Irregular in their entirety, assembled together for the first time ever. We hope you'll journey along, for between these covers, the game is always afoot....

Made in United States
Orlando, FL
29 June 2025